Marvelous Maxx
and the Bumblebee

by

John and Catherine Higgins

DORRANCE
PUBLISHING CO
EST. 1920
PITTSBURGH, PENNSYLVANIA 15238

Dorrance Publishing Co
585 Alpha Drive
Suite 103
Pittsburgh, PA 15238
Visit our website at *www.dorrancebookstore.com*

ISBN: 978-1-6453-0995-6
eISBN: 978-1-6461-0253-2

Bloomberg has snatched my chocolate bar!

He is one fast, naughty dog.

My little brother is playing ball.

Bloomberg runs toward him.

"Ethan, grab him!" I yell.

Ethan looks up.

I shout even louder, "Grab Bloomberg,
Ethan! Chocolate is toxic for dogs!"

"Toxic" means harmful. But Ethan is only
four and he doesn't know this yet.

Even so, Ethan grabs Bloomberg's tail.

Bloomberg stops in surprise and drops the chocolate. Yesss!

I pick the bar up quickly and grin. "Excellent job, Ethan!"

"Excellent" means super-good.

Ethan and I play kick.

I'm wearing my blue soccer jersey.

All of a sudden, I hear buzzing.

Oh no...

A gigantic bumblebee is chasing me!

"Gigantic" is a cool word for super-sized.

Ethan runs inside.

I flail my arms at the bumblebee.

"Flail" is a marvelous way of saying wave wildly.

But it makes no difference. The buzzing gets louder and the bumblebee zooms closer!

I sprint towards the house.

"Sprint" means run real fast!

But I can't get away quickly enough and –

"Ouch!"

The bumblebee stings me!

I crunch my teeth together and swat the buzzing stripe away.

"Swat" is a cool word for slap.

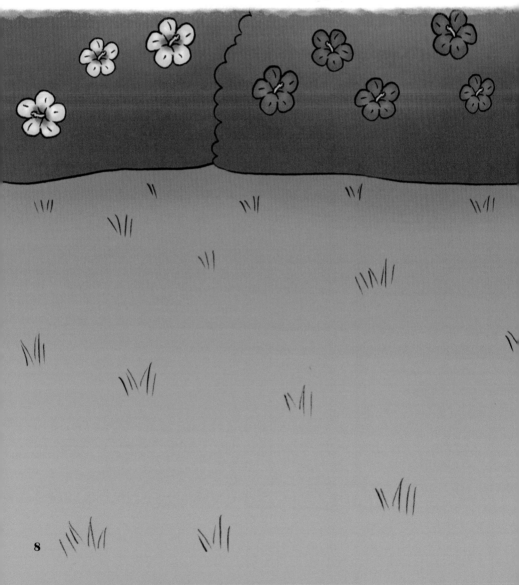

The bee has gone but the pain from the sting is intense!

"Intense" means very strong... owww!

My neck starts to itch and I feel a little out of breath.

"Mom!" I scream.

Mom runs outside.

"Maxx!" she cries. "What's wrong?"

I gulp in some air. "I think I'm allergic to bumblebee stings!" I gasp.

"Allergic" means something can make you turn red, swell up, and find it hard to breathe.

Mom looks alarmed.

"Alarmed" means worried and scared.

"You're as red as a strawberry, Maxx!" she says. "We need to get you to the doctor."

I see Doctor Z.

Doctor Z is brilliant and gorgeous.

"Brilliant" means super smart, "gorgeous" means very pretty.

Her badge says "Dr. Kristy Zhang."

"Hi, Maxx." Doctor Z smiles.

"I heard you've been fighting a bumblebee."

"Maybe." I feel a bit stupid and glance down.

"Glance" means look quickly.

"You must be very brave," Doctor Z says.

I look back up at her.

My cheeks feel warm.

"I think my blood histamine is high," I tell her.

Your body makes histamine during an allergic reaction.

Repeat after me: his-tuh-meen.

Doctor Z looks surprised. "How old are you?"
she asks.

"I just turned seven."

She gives me an even bigger smile. "Maxx,
you are wicked smart!" she says. "I hope you
know that."

Now it's not just my cheeks that feel warm.
I'm warm inside too.

Doctor Z sits down next to me. "Maxx, let's make a deal, okay?"

I nod my head. "Okay."

"If you let me give you a shot," she says, "I will give you a blue tongue depressor."

A tongue depressor is what doctors use to press your tongue down when they need to look in your throat. It's like a gigantic Popsicle stick.

I nod again. "Deal." I love all doctor things.

Doctor Z gives me the shot. It stings my arm a little.

"But not as bad as the bumblebee," I tell her.

"Wow!" Doctor Z replies. "You're tough as well as smart!"

Doctor Z gets a piece of paper from her desk.

She folds the sheet into a paper airplane and puts the tongue depressor inside.

Then she tosses the airplane towards me.

It glides through the air and lands on my lap.

"Glide" means move in a smooth motion.

I feel my face break into a huge grin.

I love the paper airplane and the tongue depressor.

"Now, Maxx," says Doctor Z. "Here are some tips so you won't get stung again."

"Bumblebees get excited when you move.

So if you hear one buzzing around, freeze
like a statue."

She points to my blue jersey.

"And believe it or not, bumblebees are attracted to blue clothes."

"Attracted" means drawn to.

"Got it?" Doctor Z asks.

"Got it," I reply.

I look in the mirror on Doctor Z's wall.

The redness on my skin has disappeared. So has the pain.

"Disappeared" means gone.

And I give Doctor Z a gigantic hug.

At home, I put the tongue depressor in my pocket. Then Ethan and I fly the airplane in our room.

Bloomberg runs in, jumps, and catches it in his mouth.

I look at Ethan. We are both exhausted, which means totally tired out.

We can't be bothered to chase Bloomberg, so we let him escape.

"Escape" is a super way to say slip away.

Mom and Dad come in.

They kiss us goodnight.

"Goodnight, Doctor Maxx. Goodnight, Ethan," they say.

I tuck my blue tongue depressor under my
pillow.

"Considering I got stung by a bumblebee," I say,
"this actually turned into a pretty cool day."

Maxx's Cool New Words

Toxic: harmful

Excellent: super-good

Gigantic: super-sized

Flail: wave wildly

Sprint: run real fast

Swat: slap

Intense: very strong

Allergic: something can make you turn
  red, swell up, and find it hard to breathe

Alarmed: worried and scared

Brilliant: super-smart

Gorgeous: very pretty

Glance: look quickly

Histamine: something made in your body
during an allergic reaction

Glide: move in a smooth motion

Attracted: drawn to

Disappeared: gone

Exhausted: totally tired out

Escape: slip away